# Happy Birthday, SpongeBob!

by J-P Chanda
illustrated by Heather Martinez

**SIMON AND SCHUSTER/NICKELODEON**

*Stephen Hillenburg*

Based on the TV series SpongeBob SquarePants created by Stephen Hillenburg
as seen on Nickelodeon

SIMON AND SCHUSTER

First published in Great Britain in 2009 by Simon & Schuster UK Ltd
1st Floor, 222 Gray's Inn Road, London, WC1X 8HB
A CBS Company

Originally published in the USA in 2005 by Simon Spotlight,
an imprint of Simon & Schuster Children's Division, New York.

A CIP catalogue record for this book is available from the British Library

ISBN  978-1-84738-584-0

Printed in Singapore

1 3 5 7 9 10 8 6 4 2

It was  birthday!

SPONGEBOB'S

July

"I hope there will be  and !" said .

GIFTS CAKE SPONGEBOB

"I love and

BALLOONS PARTY HATS

and !"

KRABBY PATTIES

"Do **you** know what day it is?"  asked .

SPONGEBOB　　　　　　GARY

"Meow?" 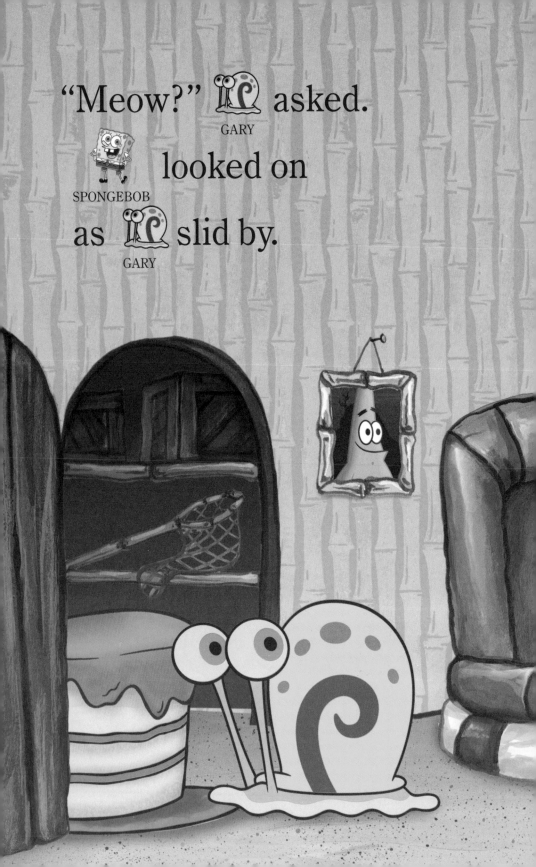 GARY asked.

SPONGEBOB looked on

as GARY slid by.

"Did  GARY forget my birthday?" wondered  SPONGEBOB .

 SANDY was pushing

a big BOX.

"Is that a GIFT?"

asked SPONGEBOB.

"No, it is my new  CHAIR,"

said SANDY.

SANDY sat on the BOX.

SANDY did not say,

"Happy Birthday."

"Do **you** know

what day it is?"

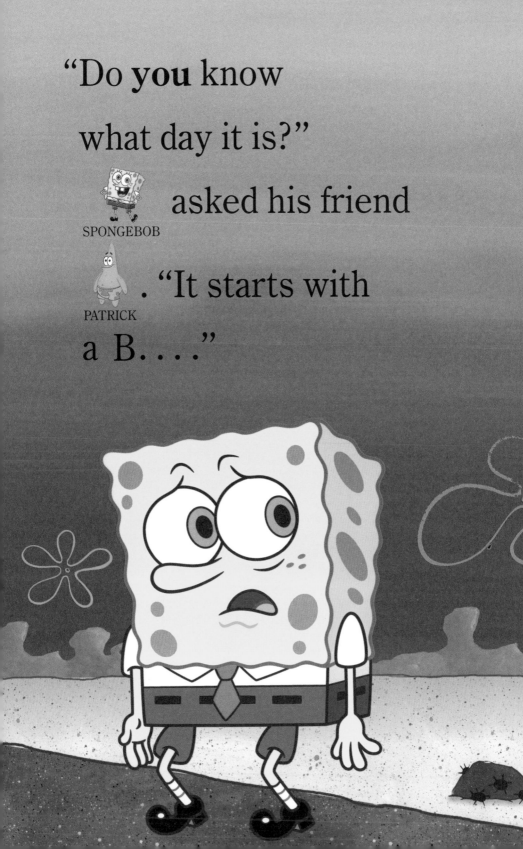 asked his friend

SPONGEBOB

. "It starts with

PATRICK

a B...."

"I know! I know!"

said  .

PATRICK

" ○ Day! 🏀 Day!

BUBBLE            BASKETBALL

🐝 Day?"

BUMBLEBEE

🧽 shook his head.

SPONGEBOB

Did everyone forget
the  and ？
GIFTS            CAKE

Did everyone forget the  and

BALLOONS

PARTY HATS

and ? 

KRABBY PATTIES

wondered .

SPONGEBOB

went to work.

The inside of the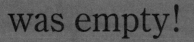

was empty!

"Hello?"  called out.

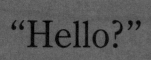
SPONGEBOB

 walked in

SQUIDWARD

and stood next to a 🪑.

TABLE

"What are you holding?"

asked 🧽.

SPONGEBOB

"This is my new wig," said  SQUIDWARD.

SQUIDWARD put the MOP on his

head.

" , do you know

what day it is?"

asked 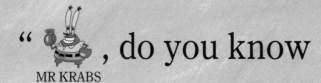 .

"It is a day to make !" said .

MONEY            MR KRABS

"Into the kitchen, !"

SPONGEBOB

"It looks like everyone

forgot my birthday,"

said  .

SPONGEBOB

"No  , no  , and

GIFTS              CAKE

no  for me."

BALLOONS

"  !" called.

SPONGEBOB     MR KRABS

"Come in here!"

"Surprise!" everyone yelled.

"Happy Birthday,  !"

SPONGEBOB

It was a big party

with  and !

GIFTS                BALLOONS

There were ...

PARTY HATS

Happy Birthday, SpongeBob!

. . . and

**KRABBY PATTIES**

with **CANDLES** on top!

"You did not forget!"

said **SPONGEBOB** . "Hooray!"